© 2001 Grandreams Books Limited.
Published by Grandreams Books Ltd.
4 North Parade, Bath, BA1 1LF. UK

Grandreams, Inc.,
4 Crossroads Drive, Suite #108, Robbinsville, NJ 08691.USA

Cinderella

ILLUSTRATED BY BRIAN ROBERTSON

Story adapted by
Christine Deverell

Once upon a time a rich gentleman who was sad after the death of his wife, decided to marry again, so his lovely daughter could have a mother to care for her.

Unfortunately he chose a proud and selfish woman with two daughters just like herself. She did not reveal her true character until after the wedding. She ordered the little girl to work in the kitchen and live with the servants, while she and her daughters enjoyed a life of splendor.

When the child had finished her work, she used to sit in the chimney corner among the cinders; so everyone called

her Cinderella. Her clothes were dirty and ragged, but she

was far prettier than her sisters in all their fine clothes.

One day an invitation arrived from the palace. The

King's son was giving a ball! The sisters could not have been happier. They talked of nothing but what they would wear, and ordered beautiful gowns from the best dressmakers in the land. Cinderella would have loved to go to the ball, and the wicked sisters teased her mercilessly saying; "Wouldn't you just love to dress up in these fine clothes and ride in a carriage to the palace, and dance with rich young men, and maybe even with the Prince himself?"

It was known that the Prince was in search of a wife, and Cinderella's mean stepmother had high hopes for her daughters. Soon, the great day arrived. Cinderella was busy

all day, dressing her sisters, polishing their shoes, combing their hair, and when the splendid carriage arrived to take them to the ball, she dutifully arranged their gowns so they would not wrinkle on the journey.

When they were out of sight, Cinderella sat down alone and exhausted in the chimney corner and began to cry. Then, all of a sudden, her Fairy Godmother appeared and said, "Why are you crying?" "I wish I could go to the ball," sobbed Cinderella. "Well then, be a good girl and do as I say. And you shall go to the ball! Run along to the garden and bring me a pumpkin."

Cinderella found the biggest and best pumpkin and

brought it to her Fairy Godmother who touched it with her

magic wand. Instantly it became a beautiful golden coach.

"Now bring me the mouse-trap, and open it very carefully."

Six mice ran out of the trap, and as the Fairy Godmother

touched each one with her wand, it turned into a fine grey

horse. Cinderella was then sent to find a rat for her Fairy

Godmother to turn into a handsome driver, and six lizards

which became smart footmen.

"Well now, will that be fit to carry a lady to the

ball?" asked the Fairy Godmother. "Oh yes. It's wonderful,"

replied Cinderella, "but . . ."

"Aha! You're wondering what you are going to wear,

are you not? Let's see; what would suit you?" With these

words, she waved her wand over Cinderella, and in an

instant her rags became the most magnificent dress you can

imagine. She was wearing the most costly jewels in the world, and on her feet was a beautiful pair of glass slippers.

"Off you go now," said the Fairy Godmother, "but mind you leave the palace before the clock strikes twelve, or all this magic will be undone."

Cinderella promised to obey, and set off in her golden carriage. When she appeared in the ballroom, everyone fell silent and the music and dancing stopped, for she was the most beautiful young woman in the room. The young Prince took her hand and led her out to dance with him. He danced with no one else the whole evening.

When they sat down to the feast, he was so busy

looking at her that he did not eat a thing! The dancing

continued. Cinderella was so happy, she had danced every dance and did not feel tired. Then she heard a clock striking the hour. "It must be 11 o'clock. It cannot possibly be midnight yet," she said to herself, remembering her Fairy Godmother's warning.

But as she turned and saw the clock, Cinderella gasped with fright and ran as fast as she could from the ballroom. The Prince tried to catch up with her as the clock continued to chime.

As she ran through the door and down the steps towards the golden carriage, she lost one of her glass slippers,

and at the very

moment that the

Prince bent down to

retrieve it, the clock

struck twelve. As he

stood up, the Prince did

not see a sign of his beautiful

dancing partner; and the coach and horses had completely

vanished.

   Behind a hedge in the garden sat poor Cinderella in

her ragged, dirty clothes. Beside her was the pumpkin. The

mice, the rat and the lizards scurried away. When she was

certain that the Prince had gone, Cinderella made her way

home on foot as fast as she could.

The music and dancing would have continued until morning, but the Prince was in no mood for celebration, and all the guests were sent away. He took the glass slipper to the King and said, "I will find the maiden whose foot this slipper fits, and when I have found her, she will be my bride."

Cinderella's stepmother grew very excited when the Prince arrived at their house. "It's only a shoe," she said to her daughters; "one of you will be able to squeeze your foot into it." But they tried in vain. It was a tiny, dainty slipper, and the sisters had big, clumsy feet.

"Are there any other young women in this house?"
asked the Prince. "Only Cinderella," said the mother, "but
she works in the kitchen, and we didn't take her to the ball."

"Bring her here," demanded the Prince. And when
Cinderella tried on the slipper everyone cried, "It fits! It
fits!" The stepmother and her
daughters were white with rage.

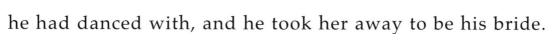

The Prince looked into
Cinderella's eyes and recognized that
she was indeed the beautiful stranger
he had danced with, and he took her away to be his bride.

They lived happily for many years in the great palace,
and the Princess, who later became Queen, was always kind
to her servants, and invited them to attend the annual ball.

21